# NORTH CAROLINA

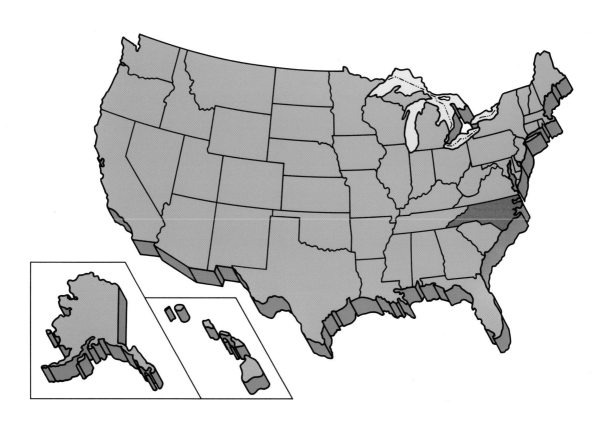

# NORTH CAROLINA

Andrea Schulz

Lerner Publications Company

LIBRARY OF CONGRESS
CATALOGING-IN-PUBLICATION DATA
Schulz, Andrea.
    North Carolina / Andrea Schulz.
        p.   cm. — (Hello USA)
    Includes index.
    Summary: Introduces the geography, history, people, industries, and current environmental issues of North Carolina.
    ISBN 0-8225-2744-8 (lib. bdg.)
    1. North Carolina—Juvenile literature. 2. North Carolina—Geography—Juvenile literature.
    [1. North Carolina.] I. Title. II. Series.
    F254.3.S38 1993
    975.6—dc20                              92-44846
                                                 CIP
                                                  AC

Manufactured in the United States of America

1  2  3  4  5  6  –  I/JR  –  98  97  96  95  94  93

Cover photograph by Frederica Georgia.

The glossary that begins on page 68 gives definitions of words shown in **bold type** in the text.

 This book is printed on acid-free, recyclable paper.

# CONTENTS

# Did You Know . . . ?

☐ The lighthouse at Cape Hatteras, North Carolina, is the tallest in the country.

☐ More denim is made in Greensboro, North Carolina, than in any other place in the world.

☐ Blackbeard, a widely feared pirate, was beheaded in 1718 at Ocracoke Inlet off North Carolina's coast. Legend says that Blackbeard's ghost still roams the coast in search of his head.

After Blackbeard was beheaded, his head was hung from a pole on a ship.

6

Orville Wright acts as test pilot, and Wilbur Wright observes the takeoff.

❑ Kill Devil Hill near Kitty Hawk, North Carolina, was the site of the world's first motor-powered airplane flight. In 1903 Orville and Wilbur Wright flew their plane a distance of 120 feet (37 meters).

❑ The world's largest frying pan is said to be in Rose Hill, North Carolina. The pan, which measures 15 feet (4.6 m) across, is used to fry more than 250 whole chickens at a time during the town's festivals.

**Rhododendron blossoms cover North Carolina's mountainsides in the spring.**

# A Trip
# Around the State

Some North Carolinians think of their state as a place of sandy beaches, grassy islands, and dark, swampy **wetlands**. Others picture a piece of hilly farmland or a busy city as home. Still other North Carolinians look out their windows and see pine-covered mountain peaks and deep valleys. Although each view is different, each is part of North Carolina.

**Bald cypress trees grow in swamplands.**

9

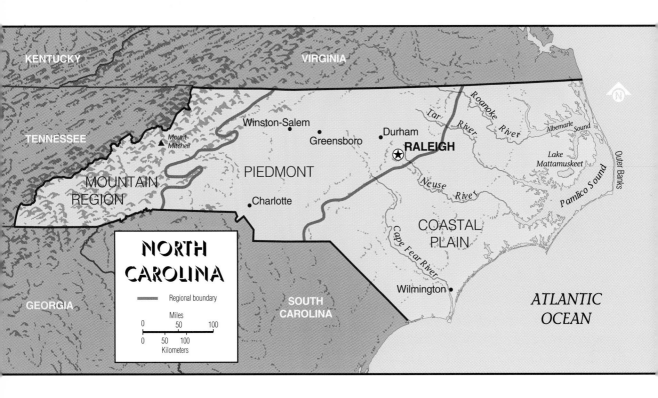

Located in the southeastern part of the United States, North Carolina is bordered on the north by Virginia. To the south lie South Carolina and Georgia. Tennessee is North Carolina's neighbor to the

The remains of an old ship rest on the shore of Cape Hatteras.

west, and the Atlantic Ocean washes up against North Carolina's entire eastern edge.

The **Outer Banks**—a long, narrow strip of sand islands just off the Atlantic coast—serve as a fragile barrier protecting North Carolina from ocean storms. Powerful ocean currents cause shifting sands, and sudden storms are common off the Outer Banks's shores. As a result, this area has witnessed many shipwrecks. The waters between the Outer Banks and the mainland are known as **sounds**. Two of the state's largest sounds are Pamlico and Albemarle.

11

North Carolina is divided into three regions—the Coastal Plain, the Piedmont, and the Mountain Region. The flat Coastal Plain covers eastern North Carolina. Marshes (grassy wetlands) and swamps (wooded wetlands), including the Great Dismal Swamp, soak part of the eastern half of the Coastal Plain. Much of the fertile land in the western half of this region is planted with tobacco and other crops. Low hills of sand roll through the southwestern part of the Coastal Plain.

**Many types of water birds make their homes in the grassy wetlands of the Coastal Plain.**

West of the Coastal Plain lies the hilly Piedmont. The two regions are separated by the **Fall Line**— an imaginary line marking the drop from the highlands of the Piedmont to the lowlands of the Coastal Plain. Rolling, wooded hills, wide fields, and most of the state's people and cities can be found in the Piedmont.

A pond in a quiet park reflects the skyscrapers of Charlotte, a city that lies on the Piedmont.

13

Layers of fog often gather over the Great Smokies.

In the Mountain Region, the Blue Ridge and Great Smoky mountain ranges cut a jagged path across western North Carolina. These two ranges are part of the Appalachians, a chain of mountains extending from Canada to Alabama. Mount Mitchell, the highest peak in the eastern United States, rises 6,684 feet (2,037 m) in North Carolina's Mountain Region.

Rivers race down from the Mountain Region and join other waterways in the Piedmont. Many of the rivers then flow through the

One of North Carolina's many waterfalls spills down a forested hill.

Coastal Plain and into the Atlantic Ocean. Some of the state's most important rivers are the Roanoke, the Tar, the Neuse, and the Cape Fear.

Most of North Carolina's lakes are artificial, formed when dams were built across the state's rivers to hold back water. Lake Mattamuskeet and a few other natural lakes can be found on the Coastal Plain.

North Carolina's temperatures vary along with its regions. The average summertime temperature on the Coastal Plain is 80° F (27° C), while the Mountain Region averages 70° F (21° C). The Coastal Plain has warmer winters, too. Temperatures there average 48° F (9° C) compared to 28° F (–2° C) in the mountains.

A generous 50 inches (127 centimeters) of **precipitation** (rain and melted snow) is measured each year in North Carolina. Most of the snow falls in the mountains.

Many different kinds of plants and animals thrive in North Carolina. Forests cover about two-thirds of the state. Pine and cypress trees grow on the Coastal Plain, and oaks, hickories, and evergreens are common in the Piedmont and Mountain regions. Flowering trees and shrubs such as azaleas, camellias, dogwoods, and rhododendrons bloom all over the state. Venus's-flytrap, an insect-eating plant, grows wild in the pine forests of the Coastal Plain.

Bears, deer, foxes, wild turkeys, opossums, river otters, and beavers make their homes in forests and along rivers throughout North Carolina. Thousands of ducks and geese spend winters in the marshes and swamps of the Coastal Plain. Wild horses gallop along a few of the islands of the Outer Banks, and loggerhead turtles lay their eggs on the islands' shores. Dolphins and whales can be spotted swimming off North Carolina's coast.

**Black bears** *(facing page, left)* **rest on a grassy hill in the Blue Ridge Mountains. A wild pony** *(facing page, right)* **scans the marsh grass on the Outer Banks, where a ghost crab** *(inset)* **digs a burrow in the coastal sand.**

# North Carolina's Story

Many thousands of years ago, the first people to enter North America crossed a land bridge that once connected the continent to Asia. As time passed, some of these American Indians, or Native Americans, traveled farther and farther south and east. Along the way, they hunted large mastodons (elephantlike animals) and beavers as big as bears. The Indians probably reached what is now North Carolina about 11,000 years ago.

**Town Creek Indian Mound** *(inset),* **which dates back hundreds of years, was explored to help scientists reconstruct these ceremonial buildings** *(above).*

19

About 3,000 years later, many of the large animals in North America died out and the Indians started hunting smaller animals such as deer and squirrels. Later tribes built villages and planted fields of corn, gourds, and squash. They also fished and gathered seeds, berries, nuts, and roots to eat. By the 1500s, several Indian tribes lived in what is now North Carolina.

A large and powerful group known as the Cherokee Nation occupied much of the area. Their homeland stretched across the mountains and valleys of the southern Appalachians. Each Cherokee village had two chiefs—one who solved daily problems and one who took charge during wars. Villagers grew many crops, including corn, beans, pumpkins, and tobacco. They shot deer with bows and arrows and caught fish with spears, traps, and hooks.

In south central North Carolina, the Catawba lived in villages of as many as 100 people. The Catawba constructed their houses using bark for

The Cherokee used hornets' nests to make booger masks. Soldiers wore the masks to make fun of their enemies during booger dances, which were held before battles.

the walls and cattails for thatched roofs. Large fields of vegetables surrounded the villages. In both Catawba and Cherokee communities, the women farmed and the men hunted.

Many Indians lived along the Atlantic coast. One group, the Tuscarora, built their villages along the Roanoke, Pamlico, and Neuse rivers. The Pamlico Indians lived to the south of the Tuscarora.

Indian women throughout what is now North Carolina were responsible for many tasks. They molded clay pots for cooking food and treated animal hides to make leather, which was cut and sewn into clothing.

**Indians living near the Atlantic coast often smoked fish over a large bonfire.**

Various groups of coastal Indians all followed similar ways of life. They hollowed out tree trunks that were 50 feet (15 m) long to make canoes for traveling and fishing. To catch fish, the men dragged nets through the water or pierced the fish with sharp spears. The women tended fields that were sometimes as large as 200 acres (81 hectares). Using frames made from wooden poles, coastal Indians built rectangular houses covered with bark or woven mats.

Coastal Indians probably greeted the area's first European visitor—Giovanni da Verrazano. An explorer hired by France, Verrazano sailed into what is now Cape Fear in 1524. Sixteen years later, Spanish explorer Hernando de Soto traveled through the area's southwestern mountains.

In the 1580s, British explorers twice tried to build **colonies**, or settlements, in what is now North Carolina. But both colonies failed. The first successful British colony was built in what is now Virginia in 1607.

**Hernando de Soto explored much of the area that is now the southeastern United States. On his journeys, de Soto captured, tortured, and killed many American Indians.**

# The Lost Colony

A group of British colonists landed on Roanoke Island in 1587. Led by John White, their governor, the settlers quickly built homes. With the help of Indians who lived nearby, the colonists gathered food in the forest. A month later, White's daughter gave birth to the first British baby born in North America—Virginia Dare.

Governor White soon had to sail back to Great Britain for supplies. When he arrived, he learned that a war with Spain had begun. All British ships were needed to fight the Spanish. White could not return to his colony until three years later.

When he finally reached Roanoke Island, Governor White found it deserted. All the colonists had disappeared. The only clue was the name of an island, "Croatoan," carved into a tree. But before White could search Croatoan Island for the colonists, a storm hit and forced him to sail out to sea.

Later searches failed to find clues to the mystery of the Lost Colony. However, some people think that the colonists joined one of the Indian tribes living near Croatoan Island (now Hatteras Island). Many of the Lumbee Indians, who live in southeastern North Carolina, have British names. Some Lumbees have blue eyes and light hair, features that may come from white ancestors. Perhaps the Lumbees' ancestors were the settlers of the Lost Colony.

**Ships arriving at Carolina's docks from Europe carried barrels of food and other goods.**

As more colonists settled in North America, Great Britain strengthened its claim on the continent. In 1663 Charles II, the British king, gave a piece of land to some wealthy friends. Called *Carolina* (the Latin name for "Charles"), the territory stretched south from the British colony of Virginia to the Spanish colony of Florida.

Soon shiploads of British people arrived in the colony of Carolina. Most of these settlers built their homes and farms near Albemarle Sound. They were soon joined by other colonists from Virginia and Pennsylvania, and by more new **immigrants** from countries such as Great Britain, Germany, Switzerland, and France.

Corn was an important food crop for both Indians and colonists.

Most of the Indians in the colony were friendly to the settlers, teaching them how to gather and plant food, as well as helping them fight unfriendly tribes. But in return, many of the settlers were not as generous. Instead, they took land from the Indians. Merchants cheated the Indians in trading. Slave traders came and kidnapped some Indians to sell as slaves in the West Indies—a group of islands south of Florida.

In 1710 a group of settlers built the village of New Bern near the Neuse River, on a piece of land stolen from the Tuscarora Indians. The Indians rebelled. Tuscarora soldiers, who were later joined by other groups of Indians, attacked white settlements near the river.

Known as the Tuscarora War, the series of battles continued for two years until the colonists defeated the Tuscarora. Most of the Tuscarora who survived the war eventually moved north to New York.

Tuscarora Indians captured two colonists and an African slave, starting what became known as the Tuscarora War. One of the prisoners later drew this picture of the trial, in which the colonists were accused of stealing Tuscarora land.

In 1712 Carolina was divided into three separate colonies—North Carolina, South Carolina, and Georgia. North Carolina was now one of thirteen British colonies on the Atlantic coast. Settlers continued to arrive in North Carolina from the other colonies, and more immigrants came from Scotland, Germany, and several other northern European countries. By the 1760s, 130,000 people were living in North Carolina.

Because they were under the rule of faraway Great Britain, North Carolina and the other twelve colonies had to follow British laws. But the colonies wanted to govern themselves. The colonists also felt it was unfair to be taxed by Great Britain. The North American colonies began planning to break away from Great Britain so they could form their own country.

The war between Great Britain and the colonies, known as the American Revolution, broke out in 1775. On July 4, 1776, representatives from all of the thirteen colonies signed the Declaration of Independence, claiming freedom from British rule. The colonies won the revolutionary war seven years later and began to organize a new nation. North Carolina joined the United States as the 12th state on November 21, 1789.

William Tryon, the British governor of North Carolina, tried to keep angry colonists from fighting against the British government in 1765.

Farmers used wooden planks to build roads for hauling hay, cotton, tobacco, and other crops to market. Many of these roads were later abandoned, after their users realized how much time and work it took to repair them.

Throughout the early 1800s, most people in central and western North Carolina worked on small farms, growing just enough food to feed their families and their livestock. Some settlers in eastern North Carolina owned **plantations**, large farms where black slaves planted and worked fields of tobacco and cotton. A smaller number of African Americans were free and had jobs as carpenters, mechanics, barbers, and tailors. Black people made up about one-third of the state's population by 1860.

# Keeping Tradition Alive

During the mid-1800s, most of the Indians of the Cherokee Nation were removed from their traditional land in the Appalachians. They were forced to go west to a reservation, or land set aside by the U.S. government for Native Americans. But about 1,000 Cherokee refused to leave their homeland. After many years of fighting for their rights, the Eastern Band of Cherokee in North Carolina was eventually allowed to govern itself. By remaining in their homeland, the Cherokee could continue to pass on their traditions and ways of life to their children and grandchildren.

**Ayunini, or Swimmer, a Cherokee leader and medicine man, helped preserve his culture by writing down ancient Cherokee traditions.**

North Carolinians near the coast made turpentine and tar from tree sap and carved tree trunks into masts. All three items were used to build ships. Fishers made a living by netting shad and herring from the state's rivers and shellfish from the coastal waters.

Workers scraped pine trees for resin, a gummy substance used to make turpentine.

The first gold discovered in the United States was found in North Carolina. Gold mining became big business in the state during the 1800s.

While Southern states such as North Carolina depended mostly on farming for money, Northerners made much of their money from manufacturing. Although many Southern plantations used slaves, slavery was illegal in Northern states, and many people wanted to make it illegal in the South as well. But Southerners argued that they needed free slave labor to earn a living.

Early in 1861, six Southern states broke away from the Union, or United States, to form a separate country—the Confederate States of America. In North Carolina, one out of four families owned slaves. Many North Carolinians did not want to join the Confederacy. But when President Abraham Lincoln sent Northern troops to keep the South in the Union, North Carolina was forced to take sides. North Carolinians did not want to fight against the South, so they joined the Confederacy at the outbreak of the Civil War.

# THE **TAR HEEL** STATE

North Carolina has been known as the Tar Heel State for a long time, but no one is really sure where the nickname came from. Tar, however, was an important part of North Carolina's economy in the 1800s.

The most common story told by Tarheels credits the state's Confederate soldiers with earning the nickname. During a difficult Civil War battle, North Carolina's soldiers were fighting side by side with troops from a neighboring state.

When the going got tough, legend says that the other Confederates ran away, leaving North Carolina's soldiers to battle the enemy alone.

When the two groups later met up, the troops who had fled teased the North Carolinians about being from a state full of tar makers. The Tarheels replied that the soldiers who fled needed some tar on their own heels to "stick" better to the next battle!

By the time the North won the war in 1865, one-fourth of all the Confederate soldiers who had been killed were from North Carolina. Many of the survivors found that their homes, farms, and crops had been destroyed. Slaves were freed, but many of them had no money, no job, and no place to live.

U.S. troops moved into North Carolina to oversee **Reconstruction**, or the rebuilding of the South. To rejoin the United States, each Confederate state had to pass a law giving African American men the right to vote. North Carolina was readmitted to the Union in 1868.

**African Americans gather to discuss an upcoming election.**

A young worker learns to examine spools of thread at a fabric mill.

The state slowly recovered from the war. Many farmers returned to planting their fields. Other people began to build cotton mills and factories for processing tobacco and making furniture. By the late 1800s, thousands of North Carolinians were busy making fabrics, cigarettes, and tables and chairs from the state's supply of cotton, tobacco, and lumber.

But the new jobs did not benefit all Tarheels. Many of the factories would not hire African Americans. Life was difficult for black North Carolinians in other ways, too. In the 1890s, state politicians passed **Jim Crow laws.** These laws prevented black people from going to the same schools as white people. They also separated blacks and

Ku Klux Klan members—who wore costumes to hide their identities—threatened, beat, and killed many African Americans and their white friends.

whites in bus stations, movie theaters, restrooms, and other public places. At the same time, lawmakers in North Carolina kept most African Americans from voting. Without voting rights, blacks had no way to change the laws.

In the early 1900s, North Carolinians worked to improve education in the state, opening nearly 160 new high schools in rural, or countryside, areas. Public libraries were established in many towns. The state also built new and better roads and highways, earning North Carolina another nickname—the Good Roads State.

North Carolina's factories grew during World War I (1914–1918) and World War II (1939–1945). Workers manufactured tons of ammunition, millions of cigarettes, and miles of fabric for uniforms to send to the soldiers fighting in Europe. The factories didn't stop after the wars, either. By 1950 North Carolinians were leading the nation in the production of towels, socks, underwear, and tobacco products.

The 1950s also marked the start of the **civil rights movement**. African Americans in North Carolina and throughout the nation banded together to fight for equal rights. The U.S. government ruled in 1954 that black students and white students must be allowed to attend the same schools. By 1960 black students in the Tar Heel State were attending what had once been all-white schools.

That same year, four black college students sat down in a whites-only restaurant in Greensboro, North Carolina, and refused to leave until they were served. Their peaceful protest grew as more and more people joined them every day. The protest finally paid off when city officials agreed to open

**White students taunt classmate Dorothy Counts** *(center)* **as she enters Harding High School in Charlotte.**

public places to both blacks and whites. Civil rights leaders all over the South began using this same method, known as a sit-in, to force public places to serve black people.

## Greensboro Lunch Counter Sit-ins

On February 1, 1960, four college students sat down and asked for coffee at a Woolworth lunch counter in Greensboro. No one would serve them, but they stayed until the lunch counter closed that evening. The students went back the next day and waited again to be served. More African Americans soon occupied 63 of the 65 seats at the counter.

By the end of the week, more than 300 students—both blacks and whites—were participating in sit-ins at various restaurants and lunch counters throughout the city. Sit-ins soon spread to other cities in North Carolina.

On July 25, 1960, the first African American was finally served at the Woolworth lunch counter in Greensboro where the sit-ins began.

By 1970 much progress had been made in North Carolina. The state's schools were teaching black students and white students in the same classrooms, and most public places were open to people of both races. Laws were passed to make sure that men and women of all races had the right to vote.

The Tar Heel State saw some big economic changes in the 1980s. Textile factories were hurt because cloth from other countries became cheaper. Some of the state's textile mills closed. The nation's demand for cigarettes dropped, as Americans learned that smoking is dangerous to their health. Tobacco growers and processors began selling much of their tobacco to other countries.

39

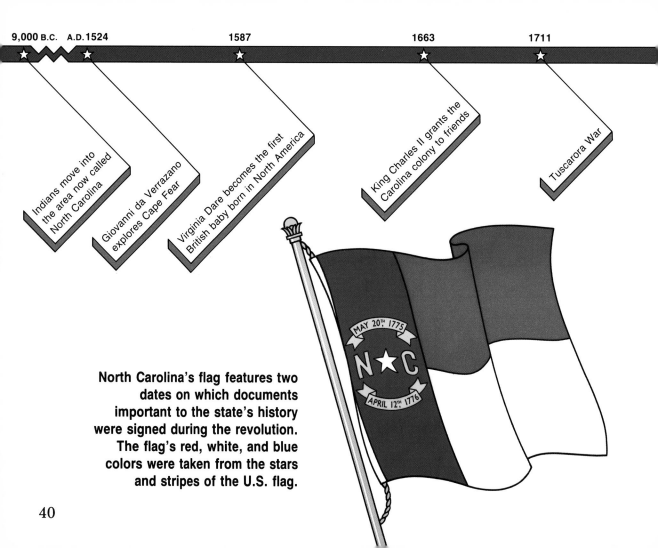

**9,000 B.C.** **A.D. 1524** 1587 1663 1711

Indians move into the area now called North Carolina

Giovanni da Verrazano explores Cape Fear

Virginia Dare becomes the first British baby born in North America

King Charles II grants the Carolina colony to friends

Tuscarora War

North Carolina's flag features two dates on which documents important to the state's history were signed during the revolution. The flag's red, white, and blue colors were taken from the stars and stripes of the U.S. flag.

MAY 20ᵀᴴ 1775
N ★ C
APRIL 12ᵀᴴ 1776

40

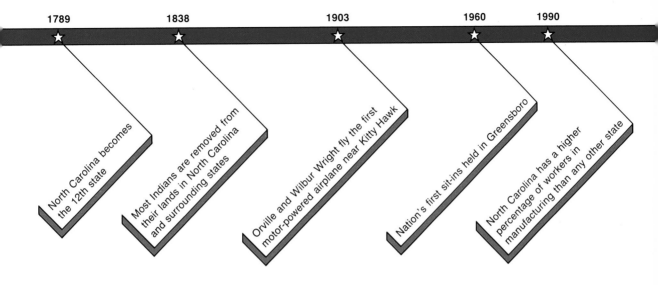

| 1789 | 1838 | 1903 | 1960 | 1990 |
|------|------|------|------|------|

North Carolina becomes the 12th state

Most Indians are removed from their lands in North Carolina and surrounding states

Orville and Wilbur Wright fly the first motor-powered airplane near Kitty Hawk

Nation's first sit-ins held in Greensboro

North Carolina has a higher percentage of workers in manufacturing than any other state

But even with these changes, the state's economy has remained strong. North Carolinians are working to attract new businesses and to create new jobs. Research Triangle Park near Raleigh, for example, has grown to be the workplace of thousands of scientists and researchers. North Carolinians still manufacture textiles, tobacco, and furniture. But nowadays they also make chemicals, computers, and telephone equipment, and have many other types of jobs as well.

# Living and Working in North Carolina

More than 6.5 million people live in North Carolina. About half of these residents live in the country or in small towns, but more and more people are moving to the state's urban centers, or cities. Some people come to study at the state's universities or to find work with new high-tech companies. Other Tarheels try starting their own businesses.

**Greensboro**

Many young North Carolinians who live in the country take care of pet horses and other animals.

North Carolina's largest cities— Charlotte, Greensboro, Raleigh (the state capital), Winston-Salem, and Durham—are in the Piedmont region. Wilmington, located on the Atlantic coast, is North Carolina's largest port city.

Almost 70 percent of all North Carolinians have ancestors from Great Britain, Scotland, Germany, and other European countries. African Americans make up 22 percent of the state's population. Small numbers of North Carolinians are Asian American or Latino.

A woman plays the bagpipe during a Scottish festival on Grandfather Mountain.

A boatbuilder demonstrates how to make a dugout canoe according to Cherokee tradition.

About 8,000 Cherokee Indians live on Qualla Boundary, a reservation in the western corner of the state. The Lumbees—believed by some people to have ancestors from North Carolina's Lost Colony—live in and around the city of Pembroke. Many Native Americans study at Pembroke State University, one of only a few colleges in the eastern United States to offer degrees in American Indian studies.

**Young visitors pan for gold at the Reed Gold Mine State Historic Site.**

Tarheels preserve their past at a variety of historical landmarks. For example, the Wright Brothers National Memorial stands near Kitty Hawk on the Outer Banks. Here, Orville and Wilbur Wright made the first motor-powered airplane flight in the world in 1903.

In Kenly, the Tobacco Museum of North Carolina traces the history of tobacco farming and processing in the state. History buffs can experience a bit of old-fashioned farm life at the Malcolm Blue Historical Farm in Aberdeen. And at the North Carolina Transportation Museum in Spencer, visitors can ride trains that have been carrying passengers for almost 100 years.

A tall man entertains North Carolinians at a county fair.

North Carolinians also celebrate many festivals. Bluegrass musicians play their fiddles and banjos at the Snuffy Jenkins Old Time and Bluegrass Music Festival in Mooresboro and at other bluegrass events around the state. Gospel singers from all over the country come to North Carolina to perform every year during their meeting in Benson. The National Hollerin' Contest, in Spivey's Corner, recalls the days when farmers talked across their fields by shouting.

47

Water lovers in North Carolina enjoy everything from rafting *(right)* to speeding down Sliding Rock *(below)*—a natural, slippery water slide.

Fishers, boaters, and swimmers enjoy North Carolina's rivers, lakes, and ocean shores. The state's mountain peaks attract hikers and downhill skiers. Adventure seekers can explore mountain caves, such as Linville Caverns. Golfers flock to North Carolina's hundreds of golf courses. In fact, they like the state so much that

Hikers in the Blue Ridge Mountains can rent tame llamas to carry packs on long trips through the rugged wilderness.

the Professional Golfers' Association located its World Golf Hall of Fame in Pinehurst.

Sports fans in the Tar Heel State cheer for the state's professional basketball team, the Charlotte Hornets. College teams—including the University of North Carolina Tar Heels, the North Carolina State Wolf Pack, and the Duke Blue Devils—also draw large crowds to their basketball games.

49

North Carolina's service workers include truck drivers and police officers.

In addition to recreation, North Carolina offers its residents a wide variety of jobs to choose from. Almost two-thirds of all working North Carolinians provide services to other people or businesses.

Some of the state's service workers are bank tellers, doctors, or clerks in stores. Many people have service jobs in the offices and laboratories of Research Triangle Park near Raleigh. Researchers there explore new ideas and products in areas including medicine, chemistry, education, electronics, and forestry.

Government service workers operate the state's public schools, military bases, and courts of law.

Soldiers at Camp Lejeune Marine Corps Base on the coast are trained to work on navy ships. Fort Bragg is where the U.S. Army's special forces are trained.

About one out of every three jobholders in North Carolina works in manufacturing—more than in any other state. The Tar Heel State continues to lead all other states in the manufacturing of tobacco products, textiles, and furniture. Greensboro has three of the world's largest textile factories. High Point's textile workers make nearly one million pairs of socks and nylon stockings every day. High Point is also known for its many furniture factories.

An electronics worker examines a computer part.

Medicines and other chemicals are manufactured in North Carolina. Some workers in the Tar Heel State assemble high-tech electronic equipment, such as computers and telephones. North Carolinians also package many food products, including meats, beverages, and baked goods.

Tobacco companies buy much of their tobacco from farmers in North Carolina. In fact, the state's farmers grow more tobacco than any other crop. North Carolina's fields of corn, soybeans, peanuts, sweet potatoes, and strawberries are also important money-makers. Two-thirds of the state's apples come from Henderson County, in the Mountain Region, where almost a million apple trees grow.

A young North Carolinian helps out during the tobacco harvest.

Farmers in North Carolina also raise chickens, hogs, and more turkeys than any other state.

Fishers haul in about $65 million worth of fish, crabs, clams, and shrimp every year from the state's rivers and coastal waters. Fish hatcheries raise catfish, crayfish, and trout in artificial ponds, and then catch and sell the adult fish.

**Fishers catch some kinds of shellfish in large, cagelike traps.**

Like many of North Carolina's waterways, the Broad River is lined with towns and farmland.

54

# Protecting the Environment

For hundreds of years, North Carolina's clean rivers and streams have been home to many kinds of plants and fish. Animals and people living near the waterways have drunk fresh, clear water and have caught plenty of healthy fish to eat. But recently, more than one-third of the state's rivers have become seriously polluted, threatening the plants and animals that are dependent on these waters for survival.

Two common pollutants in North Carolina's waterways are the chemical **nutrients** nitrogen and phosphorus. In small amounts, these nutrients help plants and animals grow. But too much of the nutrients can harm living creatures in the state's waterways.

Nitrogen and phosphorus are used to make many products, such as cleaners, dyes, and medicines. But when these chemicals are emptied down drains, they end up in household wastewater. Factories and businesses that produce or use the chemicals also discharge them into their wastewater.

Most of North Carolina's wastewater travels through pipes to sewage treatment plants. There, the water is treated to filter out chemicals and is then emptied into rivers. But many sewage treatment plants are not equipped to remove the nitrogen and phosphorus, which are then released into rivers.

Nitrogen and phosphorus also enter rivers from farmland. As ingredients in fertilizers, the nutrients are applied to crops each year to help them grow. But when farmers use too much fertilizer, rain washes the excess nitrogen and phosphorus into rivers. People in cities and towns add to the problem when they put fertilizer on their lawns and gardens. Rain then

When rainwater runs off fields, it carries away any extra fertilizer in its path.

carries any extra fertilizer into storm sewers, which empty into rivers.

When rivers are overloaded with nitrogen and phosphorus, rootless plants called algae feed on the nutrients and spread quickly over the surface of the water. Thick mats of algae keep sunlight from reaching deeper water, where plants that produce oxygen need the light to survive.

Without light, these deepwater plants die. The loss of the oxygen they produce is deadly to fish and other water animals that need oxygen to survive. The amount of oxygen in the water decreases further when the thick mats of algae die. As the algae decay, they use up even more oxygen.

**A thick layer of algae smothers a waterway.**

**Runoff from farmland turns clear waterways a muddy brown.**

The nutrients that enter rivers from farmland and from gardens are carried by sediment (soil particles that can slide into the water). Sediment is another major pollutant in North Carolina's rivers, making the water muddy and clogging the waterways. During rainstorms, soil that is washed down sloping fields and yards eventually enters streams and rivers.

Sediment also enters waterways when shopping centers, houses, and roads are built. During construction, heavy machinery is used to dig up soil. If special fences are not used, sediment can slide away from the site and clog waterways. Sediment also comes from dirt roads used to carry logs out of the forest for the lumber industry.

Sediment can fill in shallow rivers, stopping the flow of water and blocking the path of water creatures. And by making water muddy, sediment—like algae—prevents sunlight from reaching underwater plants. As the sediment settles, it coats the riverbed, smothering the plants and animals that live there.

North Carolinians are working to stop the damage to their waters. The state has passed laws to limit the amount of phosphorus and nitrogen that factories and sewage treatment plants can empty into rivers. Researchers also are developing ways to reduce the amount of nutrients in wastewater.

**Brook trout** (below) **and other fish have a hard time breathing in dirty water** (left).

Some of North Carolina's farms now collect their wastewater in holding ponds, where sediment and fertilizer can sink to the bottom. The water is then drained and allowed to enter waterways.

The state has begun working with farmers and landowners to prevent nutrients and sediment from running off North Carolina's fields, yards, and gardens. And state laws say that construction projects cannot begin without an approved plan to control the loss of sediment.

North Carolinians can help protect a waterway in their state by joining the Stream Watch program. Stream watchers learn how to spot nutrients, sediment, and other forms of pollution. Stream Watch groups also hold nature walks to teach other concerned citizens about water pollution.

When stream watchers see signs of pollution in their river, they can notify North Carolina's Department of Environment, Health, and Natural Resources. The state then tries to find the source of the pollution and begins to work on improving the river's water quality.

With new state programs aimed at fighting water pollution, North Carolinians can save their rivers from more serious damage. By working together, the state's residents hope to make their waterways clean again.

**By testing water regularly, scientists can tell when a river needs help.**

# North Carolina's Famous People

## ACTORS

**Ava Gardner** (1922–1990), from Smithfield, North Carolina, became a Hollywood star and acted in more than 20 films by the age of 28. Her most famous movies include *Showboat, Night of the Iguana,* and *East Side, West Side.*

**Andy Griffith** (born 1926) is an actor from Mount Airy, North Carolina. Griffith became famous for his starring role in the "Andy Griffith Show."

AVA GARDNER ▼

▲ ANDY GRIFFITH

## ATHLETES

**Meadowlark Lemon** (born 1932), from Wilmington, is also known as the Clown Prince of Basketball. Lemon was the star attraction for the Harlem Globetrotters from 1954 to 1978.

▼ RICHARD PETTY

MEADOWLARK
▼ LEMON

**Buck Leonard** (born 1907), a talented baseball player from Rocky Mount, North Carolina, was the first baseman for the Homestead Grays, a team in the National Negro League. As a black player, he was barred from the major leagues, which did not admit African Americans until 1947. Leonard was elected to the National Baseball Hall of Fame in 1972.

**Richard Petty** (born 1938) has won more races than any other stock-car racer in history. Petty won both the Daytona 500 and the NASCAR Winston Cup championships seven times. A museum honoring the racer is located near his boyhood home in Level Cross, North Carolina.

## BUSINESS LEADERS

**Caleb Bradham** (1866–1934), a pharmacist from New Bern, North Carolina, created the first Pepsi-Cola for dyspepsia, or indigestion. In 1902 Bradham began bottling the soft drink in the back room of his drugstore.

**Pleasant Hanes** (1845–1925), of Winston-Salem, North Carolina, launched the P. H. Hanes Knitting Company—later renamed the Hanes Corporation—in 1902, making underwear for men and boys.

**Herman Lay** (1909–1982) grew up in Charlotte and began selling potato chips out of the trunk of his car when he was 23. Six years later he bought the company that supplied the chips and renamed it H. W. Lay & Company. Lay eventually merged his business with the Frito Company to become Frito-Lay, Inc.

◄ PLEASANT HANES

ELIZABETH KOONTZ ▼

◄ CALEB BRADHAM

▲ CHARLOTTE HAWKINS BROWN

## CIVIL RIGHTS LEADERS

**Charlotte Hawkins Brown** (1883–1961) was an educator born in Henderson, North Carolina. Brown turned a run-down school for blacks in Sedalia, North Carolina, into a highly successful school that attracted the best African American students from across the country. Now called the Palmer Memorial Institute, the school is known for the success of its graduates.

**Elizabeth Koontz** (born 1919), from Salisbury, North Carolina, taught special education classes for students who needed extra help. In 1968 Koontz became the first African American president of the National Education Association, the nation's largest teachers' organization.

Floyd McKissick (1922–1991) was a respected lawyer, civil rights leader, and minister from Asheville, North Carolina. McKissick served as the national director of the Congress of Racial Equality (CORE).

▼ JOHN COLTRANE

▲ FLOYD McKISSICK

## MUSICIANS

**John Coltrane** (1926–1967) was one of the most popular jazz musicians in the 1960s. Raised in Hamlet, North Carolina, Coltrane played the saxophone and is best remembered for songs such as "My Favorite Things" and "Chasin' the Trane."

**Roberta Flack** (born 1940) grew up in Black Mountain, North Carolina. The musician's hit songs include "The First Time Ever I Saw Your Face" and "Killing Me Softly With His Song."

**Ronnie Milsap** (born 1944) from Robinsville, North Carolina, is a country musician and composer. Milsap, who has been blind since birth, is best known for hit songs such as "Any Day Now," recorded in 1982.

◄ RONNIE MILSAP

▼ ROBERTA FLACK

HOWARD
▼ COSELL

## NEWS REPORTERS

**Howard Cosell** (born 1920) began his career as a lawyer and ended up a famous sports journalist who spent 14 years on ABC's "Monday Night Football." Cosell, who is originally from Winston-Salem, retired from broadcasting in 1992.

**Charles Kuralt** (born 1934) is an award-winning broadcast journalist from Wilmington, North Carolina. Kuralt began his career as a newspaper reporter and then worked as a news correspondent for CBS. He eventually became an anchor for CBS News.

**Andrew Johnson** (1808–1875), the 17th president of the United States, was born in Raleigh, North Carolina. After serving as vice president under Abraham Lincoln, Johnson became president when Lincoln was assassinated. Johnson is the only president ever to have been impeached, or charged with misconduct while in office.

**James Polk** (1795–1849), born in Mecklenburg County, North Carolina, became the 11th president of the United States in 1844. During Polk's presidency, the nation gained about one million square miles of new territory, including what is now Texas, New Mexico, California, Arizona, and Oregon.

**Hiram Revels** (1822–1901) was the first black person elected to the U.S. Senate. Born in Fayetteville, North Carolina, Revels also opened churches and schools for African Americans throughout much of the country.

JAMES POLK ▼

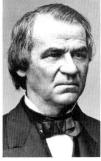

▲ ANDREW JOHNSON

HIRAM REVELS ▼

BETSY BYARS ▲

WRITERS

**Betsy Byars** (born 1928), from Charlotte, is the author of many books for children. In 1971 Byars won a Newbery Medal for *Summer of the Swans*.

**William Sydney Porter** (1862–1910), best known as O. Henry, has been called the most popular short story writer in the country. Many of his stories are funny or have a surprise ending. Two of his most famous short stories are "The Gift of the Magi" and "The Last Leaf." Porter was born in Greensboro.

65

# Facts-at-a-Glance

**Nickname:** Tar Heel State
**Song:** "The Old North State"
**Motto:** *Esse Quam Videri*
   (To Be Rather Than to Seem)
**Flower:** flowering dogwood
**Tree:** pine
**Bird:** cardinal

**Population:** 6,628,637*
**Rank in population, nationwide:** 10th
**Area:** 53,821 sq mi (139,396 sq km)
**Rank in area, nationwide:** 28th
**Date and ranking of statehood:**
   November 21, 1789, the 12th state
**Capital:** Raleigh
**Major cities (and populations*):**
   Charlotte (395,934), Raleigh (207,951),
   Greensboro (183,521), Winston-Salem
   (143,485), Durham (136,611)
**U.S. senators:** 2
**U.S. representatives:** 12
**Electoral votes:** 14

*1990 census

**Places to visit:** Biltmore Estate in Asheville, Oconaluftee Indian Village in Qualla Boundary, African Heritage Museum in Greensboro, C. Grier Beam Truck Museum in Cherryville, Tweetsie Railroad near Blowing Rock

**Annual events:** Pig Cookin' Contest in Newport (April), Hang Gliding Spectacular in Nags Head (May), Children's Day Fishing Tournament in Durham (June), Sand Sculpture Contest in Ocracoke (July), North Carolina Oyster Festival in Shallotte (Oct.)

| **Average January temperature:** 41° F (5° C) | **Average July temperature:** 70° F (21° C) |
|---|---|

**Natural resources:** soil, feldspar, kaolin, gneiss, lumber, water, clay, mica

**Agricultural products:** tobacco, corn, soybeans, turkeys, hogs, chickens, eggs, apples, dairy products, peanuts, sweet potatoes

**Manufactured goods:** tobacco products, textiles, chemicals, electrical equipment, machinery, food products, furniture

ENDANGERED SPECIES
**Mammals**—red wolf, Virginia big-eared bat, northern flying squirrel, eastern cougar
**Birds**—peregrine falcon, red-cockaded woodpecker, bald eagle, ivory-billed woodpecker
**Reptiles**—eastern tiger salamander, loggerhead
**Fish**—shortnose sturgeon, Cape Fear shiner
**Plants**—Michaux's sumac, small-anthered bittercress, Canby's cowbane, mountain sweet pitcher plant, rough-leaf loosestrife

WHERE NORTH CAROLINIANS WORK
**Services**—50 percent
   (services includes jobs in trade; community, social, & personal services; finance, insurance, & real estate; transportation, communication, & utilities)
**Manufacturing**—27 percent
**Government**—15 percent
**Construction**—5 percent
**Agriculture**—3 percent

AGR 3%
CONST 5%
SERVICES 50%
GOVT 15%
MFG 27%

## PRONUNCIATION GUIDE

Albemarle  (AL-buh-mahrl)

Catawba  (kuh-TAW-buh)

de Soto, Hernando  (deh SOH-toh, ehr-NAHN-doh)

Hatteras  (HAT-ur-uhs)

Neuse  (NOOS)

Piedmont  (PEED-mahnt)

Raleigh  (RAH-lee)

Roanoke  (ROH-uh-nohk)

Tuscarora  (tuhs-kuh-ROHR-uh)

Verrazano, Giovanni da  (vehr-raht-SAHN-oh, joh-VAHN-nee dah)

# Glossary

**civil rights movement**  A movement to gain equal rights, or freedoms, for all citizens—regardless of race, religion, or sex.

**colony**  A territory ruled by a country some distance away.

**Fall Line**  A line that follows the points at which high, rocky land drops to low, sandy soil. Numerous waterfalls are created along this line when rivers tumble from the upland to the lowland.

**immigrant**  A person who moves to a foreign country and settles there.

**Jim Crow laws**  Measures that separate black people from white people in public places, such as schools, parks, theaters, and restaurants. Jim Crow laws were enforced in the U.S. South from 1877 to the 1950s.

**nutrient** A material that serves to nourish, or feed, a living plant or animal.

**Outer Banks** Long, narrow strips of sandy land off North Carolina's coast, separated from the mainland by a body of water. The banks of sand can shift and change in shape.

**plantation** A large estate, usually in a warm climate, on which crops are grown by workers who live on the estate. In the past, plantation owners often used slave labor.

**precipitation** Rain, snow, and other forms of moisture that fall to earth.

**Reconstruction** The period from 1865 to 1877 during which the U.S. government brought the Southern states back into the Union after the Civil War. Before rejoining the Union, a Southern state had to pass a law allowing black men to vote. Places destroyed in the war were rebuilt and industries were developed.

**sound** A long inlet of water next to a coast, generally separating the mainland from an island or group of islands.

**wetland** A swamp, marsh, or other low, wet area that often borders a river, lake, or ocean. Wetlands support many different kinds of plants and animals.

69

# Index

**Acknowledgments:**

John R. Patton, pp. 2–3, 14; Maryland Cartographics, pp. 2, 10; North Carolina Department of Cultural Resources, Division of Archives and History, Historic Sites Section, pp. 19 (top & inset), 21, 46; Library of Congress, pp. 7, 23, 35, 65 (top left & top right); © Danny Dempster, pp. 8, 17 (left & inset); Jerry Hennen, pp. 9, 11, 26, 47, 48 (bottom); © Brent Parrett / NE Stock Photo, p. 12; Frederica Georgia, pp. 13, 42, 43, 44, 49, 52, 69; Mary A. Root / Root Resources, p. 15; North Carolina Department of Travel & Tourism, pp. 17 (right), 48 (top), 71; © Adam Jones, p. 18; North Carolina Division of Archives and History, pp. 22, 25, 27, 30, 32, 33, 36, 37, 63 (bottom right), 65 (bottom left); Independent Picture Service, pp. 24, 64 (top left); North Carolina Collection, University of North Carolina Library at Chapel Hill, pp. 29, 63 (bottom left); National Anthropological Archives / Smithsonian Institution, p. 31; *The Charlotte Observer*, p. 38; *Greensboro Daily News and Record*, p. 39; Loren M. Root / Root Resources, p. 45; Dare County Tourist Bureau, p. 53; © Charles Gupton / Picturesque, p. 50; © Chip Henderson / Picturesque, p. 51; Jennifer Larson, p. 54; © W. A. Banaszewski / Visuals Unlimited, p. 56; © John D. Cunningham / Visuals Unlimited, p. 57; © William J. Weber / Visuals Unlimited, p. 58; Iredell Soil and Water Conservation District and USDA, Soil Conservation Service, Statesville, NC, pp. 59 (left), 60, 61; © Gerry Lemmo, p. 59 (right); Hollywood Book & Poster Co., pp. 62 (top left & top right), 64 (bottom left); Daytona International Speedway, p. 62 (bottom left); Harlem Globetrotters, p. 62 (bottom right); Sara Lee Corp., p. 63 (top left); National Education Association, p. 63 (top right); Atlantic Records, p. 64 (top right); Michelle Broussard, p. 64 (center); Milton Blumenfeld, p. 64 (bottom right); Ed Byars, p. 65 (bottom right).